PJMASKS

PJ RIDERS TO THE RESCUE!

Based on the episode "PJ Riders"

Simon Spotlight

New York London Toronto Sydney New Delhi

PJ Masks © 2022 FrogBox/Ent. One UK Ltd/Hasbro.
Based on the original books by Romuald *Les Pyjamasques* © 2007 first published in France by Gallimard Jeunesse.

SIMON SPOTLIGHT

An imprint of Simon & Schuster Children's Publishing Division. 1230 Avenue of the Americas, New York, New York 10020
This Simon Spotlight paperback edition December 2022. Adapted by Maria Le from the series PJ Masks

For information about special discounts for bulk purchases, please contact Simon & Schuster Special Sales at 1-866-506-1949 or business@simonandschuster.com.
Manufactured in the United States of America 1122 LAK • 2 4 6 8 10 9 7 5 3 1 • ISBN 978-1-6659-2598-3 • ISBN 978-1-6659-2599-0 (ebook)

Greg, Amaya, and Connor cannot believe that every PJ Masks vehicle has been stolen by speed-obsessed twins, Carly and Cartoka! How can they save the day without their vehicles? "At least we still have our trusty old bikes!" says Greg.

They walk toward Greg's driveway and are shocked by what they find. The bikes are still there, but the wheels are missing!

"Stolen by those sneaky machine thieves again!" says Connor.

What are the PJ Masks going to do without any vehicles?

"What about our PJ Riders?" Amaya asks.

Maybe their new animal friends can help them get their vehicles back from Carly and Cartoka!

PJ MASKS, WE'RE ON OUR WAY! INTO THE NIGHT TO SAVE THE DAY!

Greg becomes Gekko!

Amaya becomes Owlette!

Connor becomes Catboy!

THEY ARE THE PJ MASKS!

The PJ Masks arrive at HQ, and the PJ Crystal shines brightly. They are ready to call on the PJ Riders!

"By the power of speed!" Catboy says.

"By the power of flight!" adds Owlette.

"By the power of a lizard's might!" Gekko shouts.

Cat Stripe King, Eagle Owl, and Power Lizard burst from the glowing emblems on the PJ Masks' hero costumes.

The PJ Masks put on their helmets. They are ready to ride!

"We need to get our vehicle parts back!" says Catboy. Cat Stripe King stretches and pounces around instead.

"Swoop and pick me up!" says Owlette, but Eagle Owl flaps her wings and flies up without Owlette.

"Let's go!" Gekko says to Power Lizard. Power Lizard stomps his feet and makes the ground shake.

Suddenly the three animals rush out of HQ. The PJ Masks cannot control the PJ Riders!

"Maybe we need to train them," Catboy says.

"Sit!" Owlette says.

Eagle Owl flies into the sky, Cat Stripe King sprints into the woods, and Power Lizard knocks down trees. They will not listen to the PJ Masks! Catboy droops with disappointment.

"No vehicles. No Riders. No hope," he says.

Off in the distance Carly and Cartoka spy on the PJ Masks. They watch as PJ Robot whistles and beeps for the PJ Riders to go back inside HQ.

"Do you see that?" asks Carly.

"Of course. That robot could be a battery for our Flashcar! Ultimate power, ultimate speed!" Cartoka says.

At HQ, the PJ Masks brainstorm on how they can work together with the PJ Riders.

"Maybe we should try listening to them," Owlette says.

Then Gekko spots something on the monitor. "Look! Carly and Cartoka are on the loose!"

The PJ Masks watch the screen as the twins steal tires from a car and bring them to the Flashcar.

"Our PJ vehicle parts! The whole Flashcar is made out of them!" says Catboy.

"PJ Riders, we need you!" Catboy shouts.

Catboy lassos on to Cat Stripe King, Owlette clings on to Eagle Owl, and Gekko holds on to Power Lizard's horns. The PJ Masks can barely hang on as the PJ Riders run toward the city.

"Our vehicles were so much easier to control!" says Gekko.

The PJ Riders run and fly at full speed, but then they suddenly skid to a stop. The PJ Masks fly off and tumble onto the ground.

"Fluttering feathers!" says Owlette as she crashes into Catboy.

Owlette, Catboy, and Gekko watch as the PJ Riders hoot, snarl, and roar.
"What's wrong?" asks Owlette.
The PJ Riders pace around and turn to run away in the opposite direction.
"We have to go that way to catch Carly and Cartoka!" Gekko tells them, but the PJ Riders will not listen.
"Hey! If you can't listen, then go back into the pajamas," Catboy says.
The PJ Riders zip back into the bright glow of the pajama emblems.

The PJ Masks wonder how they can catch Carly and Cartoka without the PJ Riders.

"I guess we'll have to walk," says Gekko.

The three heroes slowly make their way on foot. When they finally catch up, Carly is ready to zoom away with the Flashcar.

"We're here to take back our PJ parts!" says Catboy.

"You can't catch me without your animals," says Carly. She slams on the accelerator and the Flashcar speeds away.

"Look!" Owlette says. She sees the Flashcar's tire tracks. "Carly is headed for HQ!"

The PJ Masks have no choice but to head to HQ on foot.

Cartoka throws a pebble at HQ's window and waits. PJ Robot comes out to inspect the noise.

"Maximum magnet power!" Cartoka shouts. He uses the Gigantogarage magnet and captures PJ Robot! Carly skids up to the Gigantogarage with the Flashcar.

"We've got ourselves a new battery!" Cartoka tells her.

Catboy, Owlette, and Gekko finally reach HQ and see PJ Robot attached to the Flashcar.

"You can take our PJ vehicle parts, but you can't take our friend!" Owlette says.

"You can't catch us!" says Carly as she speeds away. Cartoka zooms after her in the Gigantogarage, and the two disappear into Zoomzania with a bright flash.

"Wriggling reptiles! That's why the PJ Riders tried to run away earlier. They sensed PJ Robot was in trouble!" says Gekko.

"We should have listened to them," Catboy says. "Maybe they'll give us a second chance."

"Cat Stripe King!" Catboy shouts.

"Eagle Owl!" says Owlette.

"Power Lizard!" Gekko calls. The PJ Riders burst from the PJ Masks' pajama emblems.

"We're sorry we didn't listen," Gekko says.

"You're not just a ride. You're our friends, too," says Owlette.

The PJ Riders listen calmly. They nod their heads and let the PJ Masks pet them softly.

"Will you help us rescue PJ Robot?" Owlette asks.

Cat Stripe King, Eagle Owl, and Power Lizard all crouch down. Then the PJ Masks' emblems shine brightly. Their suits light up and transform into body armor!

"Cool! New riding armor!" says Owlette.

"PJ Masks and PJ Riders to Zoomzania!" Gekko says.

"How do we get to Zoomzania?" Owlette asks.

"You just go really fast," says Catboy.

Cat Stripe King sprints, Eagle Owl swoops, and Power Lizard speeds faster than they ever have before. The PJ Masks and PJ Riders enter the Zoomzania portal with a flash of light.

In Zoomzania, the PJ Masks see Carly and Cartoka in the Flashcar with PJ Robot.

"Look out, speed twins!" says Gekko. Power Lizard lunges after the Flashcar, but he isn't fast enough. Catboy and Cat Stripe King chase after Carly, but the Flashcar speeds up even faster.

Owlette and Eagle Owl swoop down to try to pick up PJ Robot, but Carly swerves the Flashcar away. PJ Robot's power makes the Flashcar too fast for the PJ Riders to catch!

The PJ Masks stop for a break. Cat Stripe King growls, Eagle Owl hoots, and Power Lizard roars.

"They are trying to tell us something," Owlette says.

"Maybe they have an idea. PJ Riders, you take the lead!" Gekko says.

"It's time to be heroes!" says Catboy.

Cat Stripe King chases after the Flashcar and runs alongside it.

"Zoom, zoom, zoom!" Carly says. She turns the Flashcar around and speeds off in the opposite direction.

Power Lizard runs to the end of a tunnel and blocks the exit. Carly slams on the brakes and turns the Flashcar around again. Then Eagle Owl swoops down.

"Super Owl Wing Wind!" Owlette shouts.

Eagle Owl flaps her wings and sends a powerful gust of wind at the Flashcar. The Flashcar flies up and into the muddy bog!

"We're stuck!" says Carly.

Owlette and Eagle Owl swoop down and pick up PJ Robot from the Flashcar.

"Hey, give me back our battery!" says Cartoka.

"Not a chance! We'll take back our PJ vehicle parts too!" says Catboy.

Cat Stripe King leaps forward, but Carly slams the accelerator and finally frees the Flashcar from the muddy bog.

Carly and Cartoka escape and speed away.

The PJ Masks and PJ Riders watch as the twins zoom away in the Flashcar again.

"We can chase down our vehicle parts another night," says Gekko.

"For now, we have the PJ Riders and PJ Robot. Our friends and allies," Owlette says. Cat Stripe King roars, Eagle Owl hoots, and Power Lizard growls in cheer.

PJ Masks and PJ Riders all shout hooray! Because in the night, they saved the day.